Almost Everyone

Thomas Timmins

Poems

ISBN: 978-0-9975112-3-9
Printed in United States of America

Published by Zoëtown® Media
Zoëtown is registered trademark of Zoëtown Media.
Greenfield, MA
www.thomastimmins.com

Book design by Maureen Moore,
Ginger Cat's Booksmyth Press
www.thebooksmythpress.com

Dedication

To Barbara whose joy in life and riotous humor uplifts us and everyone she meets, and that's a lot of people

To Betty whose sweetness of spirit and dedication to others makes us all feel loved and deeply cared for

OTHER BOOKS BY THOMAS TIMMINS
www.thomastimmins.com

Novels
> *The Hour Between One and Two (Trilogy)*
>> *Blood Medicine*
>> *The Special Fruit Company*
>> *Down at the River*
> *Aphrodisiac for an Angel*

Short Fiction
> *Puff of Time*
> *Visions of My Other Self*
> *Desert Dusk Music*

Graphic Verse Novel
> *Zom*

Poetry
> *I Was Just Laughing*
> *Likings for Shadows*
> *Food Breaks Free*

LIST OF POEMS

Almost everyone

Weather talk

Buddhist Breathing in America

Almost everyone

Waiting

Can a poem
wait for a reader
the way a cardinal waits singing
for snow to melt in spring?

If it's so
a poem waits,
a cardinal sings.

What we want to see

The best we can do
is to hop on
the merry-go-round
of what we see
and ride its shiny animals
up and down,
all around
a little circle
outside of town.

If we climb off our painted tigers and
dragons,
step onto the dusty ground,
stroll toward places we've never been
before,
our legs wobble,
we blink in the new light,
the carousel organ tunes grow distant,
and the best we can do is wonder
what now?
There's a tree.
Let's go sit under it
to wait and see
what comes along.
Look, there's a pony.
Hey, I think I recognize
that blue dragon.
Yeah, those yellow eyes,
that spiky tail.
Yeah, I know that dragon.

Friendship

My friend and I sat on the berm
at the south end of Weatherhead Hollow pond.
I closed my eyes against the late Sunday sun
when I heard the splash.
Was that a fish? I asked my friend. I don't know,
he said, I was watching the orange kayaks
at the upper end of the pond.
I thought they might get caught in the weeds.
That's all right, I said. It's good you had your eyes
open when mine were closed. Yup, he said,
it's what friends are for. One keeps his eyes open
while the other dreams. You could say
one is a dreamer and the other is a watcher, I said.
Just then, another splash.
Did you see that one? I said. No, but I heard it.
The orange kayaks arrived at our end of the pond.
Their two-bladed paddles splashed the water
like a chorus of fish
jumping and flopping back in a slow rhythm.

Essay against slavery

In the olden days of the Celts in Ireland, a poet was equal to a king in his honor price.

This was when any woman's honor price was exactly half her husband's.

If you dishonored a king by insulting his perfection, or a poet by refusing to pay his fee in beer or a feast, or a shaman by disturbing his ritual,

for each insult, you paid them seven cumal, young women who of course could bear them babies and assure their immortality in the stories in the mouths of those babes and the face of the father carried down the generations.

This practice lasted until about 600 CE. By then there weren't enough girls to go around, so the lawyers changed the rules: 7 cumal were valued at 21 cattle.

Today, 21 little bulls raised outside Tlapacoya in rural Mexico sell for about $5,000 though revenge for an insult can cost far less.

Today, a woman is priceless. Anyone who puts a price on her life is a slaveholder. Slavery of any kind anywhere anytime curses humanity.

Slavery is the original human stain because it kills the slave, whether or not she or he breathes, walks, eats, talks, dreams.

I hate slavery.

In the heart of slavery, human destruction lurks.

Love and uniting with others to end hated
slavery is how hate can fuel love.

I hate slavery.

Coyote girls

Coyote yowls
tinged with pain
and joy
rise and trail into echoes among the trees.

Why do coyotes howl?

Celebrate their kill?

Praise the taste?

Lament the scant spoils of the hunt?

It's the females of the species, you know,
who hunt.

Calling for a mate?

It's the pack of females, you know,
who tend the pups.

At dusk, coyote voices
flare up in the ears of all who can hear.

Don't their wails
warn the other animals
of their predatory presence?

The coyotes' howls
are nothing new to the other creatures
of the forest.

The way of the woods comes down to
a matter of wits:
Who feeds is
who lives.

As night swallows the day's last light,
the coyote girls
sing the pleasures and perils of the night.

Belief

Because I believed him when
he said it doesn't matter
after all, I stayed in the shadows
of the forest of images and vinous
sentences striving for light
above rooted feelings and blossoms
I never intended,

and I believed him, so I never
took up the macheté, not for fear
of blisters on my hands
or too much sun
but that, too,

no, I left the rampant growth alone
for the love of green and grazing sounds,
branches clacking in breeze, nuts pinging,
birds I can never name
trilling at dawn, then late,
crickets teasing dusk
under splattering raindrops ...

all of what requires not pruning
or testament,
only presence.

Bzz. Bzz. Bzz.

Fly, get out of my bedroom.

Not now, you say?

Then I'll open the door,
switch on the hall light
and shut off my reading lamp.

OK, you say.
It's warmer out there in the hall.

Fine with me, I say.
Good night, good riddance.

Silence.

Divination

I'm learning divination.
My teacher is bodiless & he might
be a she & she might not even
exist. It's been roughly a lifetime
since I began my studies. The first
thing I predicted with real accuracy was
the war would end. Then, nineteen
years ago, I foresaw the end of television
as we knew it. Yesterday, I forecast
the return of the living souls of John Lennon,
Jack and Bobbie, Martin, Joan of Arc,
Eleanor Roosevelt, Mary Lincoln,
& Grandma Moses. I predicted they'd
be the first team of pioneers weightless enough
and fearless enough to fly across space
in the hydrogen fueled ship named "Rarin' to Go"
and settle Mars. They would bring a premium on
social harmony and beauty. Along
with them, a herd of nanobot puppies
will handle the material realms, but the real
nanopup job will be to transform themselves
into guitars, drums, microphones, amps
& speakers for live concerts broadcast
throughout the galaxy. The concerts were
part of the deal the government will
make with Lennon. The rest
of the team will be happy to have another
shot at life, but John will say "I'll only do it
if we can sing *Give Peace Chance* on
Sundays, *Imagine* on Tuesdays, &
Number 9 whenever we
feel like it & I want 10 billion
listeners." The government will

nod, and John will say, "I want Yoko, too."
When they tell him she's still alive but
too old to fly in a space ship, he'll say
"All right. Peace will be enough for now."

Elegy for Matthew

For 20 years, Matthew ran the Thursday evening
community meal for the ever-growing numbers of poor
in his little town. He was dedicated to making sure
everyone had their fill of good food and neighborly care.

On nights of meatloaf, mashed potatoes and gravy,
creamed corn, with dessert of a thick brownie
under vanilla ice cream, the dining room overflowed
with the hungry of all ilks and shapes. Matt hated
to travel if it meant missing a community meal.

During the weekdays, he sculpted fantasy beings
by gluing and bolting plastic scraps and junk metal.
He gave every one of hundreds a poignant name:
Dog boy. Aristotle. Mophead. Sweet Pea. Tricksee.
Queen Kate. Dear Jack. Rock Star.

When he died, his studio became an orphanage for
half-formed humanoids. Under the tables and benches
lay plastic spoons, ballpoint pen casings, shredded
six-pack nets, fan blades, shiny ball bearings all heaped
like hard-boiled Easter eggs waiting for their dipping.

Before he died, Matthew told me sometimes he heard
in the studio silence ghostly moans from the pipes,
gratings and rustlings from the walls sounding
like pleas by spirits demanding to be born right away.
 Why did they need bodies of metal and plastic?
They insisted it was the being alive that mattered,
not the stuff they dressed their souls in.

Matt agreed. After all, he was there to serve.

So he picked up his wrenches and glue gun
and went to work.

Avocado for breakfast

She reached across the banisters to pluck
a fat avocado hanging still as an oval dark moon.
Losing her balance, she clung to the fruit
that gripped her hand like a fireman

as she leaned back hard, avocado in her palm
for a moment before it flew up into soft sky
while she sat down, skirt spread wide as
a rescue sheet waiting for the fruit to fall back to her

quiet as a sighing guitar when early morning sun
casts pale shadows through the green limbs,
calm again after the sudden jiggle and rush
when her hand tugged a stem

she never expected to resist this late in the season

and now, after the avocado lands in her lap,
she lies back on the deck,
blue light filling her eyes.

Sacred the concerns of the self

How the concerns of the self
feel universal, immense, dominant,
even sacred as if one life
were the embodiment of all life,
as if life force infusing the self
was the original impulse
carried on with the purpose of
satisfying my incomparable human
needs, assuring identity
not only survives but flourishes
in every nerve cell of the body, every wish
in the mind, every inkling & fear &
demand of the heart, because
no blinking, no second thoughts
are ever needed, no other's opinion matters,
friendly or contrary,
only that prayers be always answered
as they are, immediately,
even if the self doesn't know it
at the time,
whether prayed for the love
& well-being of beloveds or
for the self's own exaltation into
rapturous realms that must exist because
the self tasted them once
& bristling with the frisson of super-
oxygenated blood like this morning's
levitation into tender green leaves
overhead, when every notion,
every emotion
soaked in happiness, complete as
the self can imagine, on this earth,
or in any world that is, was, or will be.

Beauty is a pleasure

Beauty is a pleasure
rarely recognized
even tho
all we have to do
is look
with the looking
that takes no clock time,
only heart time,
and beauty
soaks us and
all we have to do
is feel it
all the time.
Beauty smells divine.
Eyes open and alert,
take a deep breath now.
Ahhhhhh ...

Now can't exist

It's always much later than it should be.

Now it's 11:12 p.m., Cinco de Mayo,
already. Some people are dying,
including my parents, it's clear.
The time will come soon, they know, I know,
it would be useless to say no, so I say no,
& I mean it. But what I really mean is
no, stop this slow grinding down of the bodies.
Hopeless to say it. Why bother? Proud?

My dad's played his last 9 holes, he's
made his last sale to a happy
new homeowner,
the condo on the golf course, close to
the tiny airport, beside the lake
where for years my mother
threw Christmas-in-July parties
for her grandkids,
with a tree and bulbs and lights and presents
and colored lights strung across the ceiling
and doors and windows of the cottage porch
people driving by would slow down to look at.

So many things linger
in the mysterious universe we call the past
where my mother will never cook another
Sunday roast beef with carrots and onions
and baked potatoes and butter and salad,
then it was margarine
she thought was healthier for my dad to eat,
and it must have been because she fed him

and kept him alive, and he's still living, if now
only by the grace of oxygen, nitroglycerin,
and his own love and happiness, sleeping across
the long hall from his wife in the nursing home
where she finally got a TV to watch cooking shows
she always watched, so some part of the day
is familiar, happens again and again, happens
now, even if what now I can never touch again
no longer exists.

If you think about it,
now doesn't exist.
It can't. It's not a time.
Only always can exist.
Only always exists.

The second oldest poem in the world

Plug your ears.

Listen for a while.

Now, can you remember
the first poem in the world?

The idealist blogs

The idealist labored,
in his way, for months
to bring forth
a book with a new idea that would
simplify
the way people got things done,
let them lose their fears,
brace their self-confidence
so peace between neighbors
wasn't a fence-mending thing
but a hey, try my new heirloom tomato
and, sure I'll pick up your brother
from the airport at dawn,
always keeping friendliness in mind
but with a constant free-lance disinterest
in the bastard down the hill
between his house and the sea
who grew giant bamboo
no matter who's view got clobbered.

The idealist learned
he had three months to live
and the book would take
at least another year to finish.

So he decided to turn it into a
100-day blog,
write one complete sentence every day,
add whatever meaningful blather
he could manage,
and c'est la vie,
c'est la mord.

He aimed his eyes above
the topmost leaves of the bamboo,
bathed them in blue,
and scheduled his departing flight
for 100 days from now,
but wait till after sunrise tomorrow,
he said to himself,
I'll start writing then, goddamit.

But he started typing right away.
I gotta practice,
he said, almost praying,
at least I've got time
to write the first draft.

The idealist praises solar panels

This morning's
blue sky,
paler than yesterday's,
doesn't mean a thing
except another day
of beautiful drought,
a sky
people in Beijing
might stare up into
in a minute of awe
remembering the old days,
believing perhaps
in a modern miracle
greater than a job,
more powerful than money
or human brains,
the blue miracle of
21st century smokestack scrubbers
and solar panels with batteries
and electricity arriving
without a trail of smoke.

The idealist prays

Having learned
at a young age
his efforts
would have little to do with
making the world
a better place,

he fathered children,
one after the other,
in the years before
the low sperm count epidemic,

and every day after
the birth of the first,
he tipped a splash
of his wine onto the ground
in offering to
the god of luck
for his children's happiness

thereby enlisting help
for turning his idealism
into something more powerful
than dreams
that could come true
if the good genes held
and the black swans stayed in Australia.

Beannacht for Estelle on her 100th birthday

The day the garden seems a mile away
and your walker won't roll because
its tires went flat,
may a Pacific breeze lift and fill the sails
of your heart with the soothing grace of waves.

At 3 a.m. when you wake up
fearing you've missed the day
and your aching back feels like
you'll never move again,
may you remember what your doctor says
every time he listens to your heart,
"You're going to be here at least five more years."
So, you roll over and rise up for another day
of surprise visits and bright conversations.

When the memory of that narish Izzy Shapiro
who abandoned your beauty and wit
and true love seventy years ago
for the homely woman whose father was rich
because his mother told him to,
may the spirit of your 39 year marriage
to Harry surround you with the everlasting love
of a real man for a real woman.

When the lines in the book smear together
and the light coming in the window grows dim,
when music sounds like pans clattering
in the kitchen, and Oprah makes no sense at all,
may you read in the eyes of your daughter
the epic poem that begins and ends,
"Don't worry, mom.
I'll take care of you."

Though your grandchildren live far away
and you never learned to drive,
and your oldest friends and sisters are gone
or can't travel to see you any more,
may everyone you've ever loved pass through
your memories with smiles on their faces
and may you feel their warm kisses
touch your cheek.

In your hundredth year as the money
swirled down the drain
and even the two-for-one sales
are no bargain,
may everything else in life
be a mitzvah, kinahora.

When the food tastes like mush at breakfast,
lunch, and dinner, and you can do without
the chocolate and the snacks,
may you feast on the friendship
of your friends of all ages,
and savor the care of your family who journeys
across the continent to celebrate you.
May you taste on your lips the sweetness
of the love and happiness of your girls
and may you always count on relaxing
in the warmth of your lined red coat
and the elegance of your good black slippers.

Can't stop

I can't stop opening doors for wrinkled women
who may already be junior to me
so who am I to say what old is
especially at the post office
where the women ask for
a sheet of bird stamps, please,
and at the library
where they disappear up the stairs
for the gala nobody advertised
and of course at the bank
where I'm transferring my rent payment
to my landlord's new account
while the soft old beautiful women check on their
savings account balances
and I imagine their ancient tea sets
brought back from old Bangkok
adorning their kitchen windowsills
under gray northern light and there
my imagination fails
and again and again
I can't help myself so I open
the library doors for myself
for a quick visit to my brothers, my sisters,
my competitors,
my personal entertainers,
my teachers,
and cultivate my
one-sided friendships with them
until I'm tempted to check out a book,
a CD, but never a DVD even tho
movies are the most popular library borrowings
these days, and I ask myself, my imagination
revived, is checking out a book

preparing me, giving me practice for
checking out of this scene?
I'm hooked on
acting out my script so is that why I
practice checking out again and again,
to shine my chops and make my marks
without even trying?

Later I tell my daughter I hang out in libraries
and bookstores like an alcoholic hangs out
in bars and she says
I can see that.

Beannacht for Claude and Shirley on your 67th wedding anniversary

On the day the walk to the mailbox
feels like a mile run at top speed,
may warm prairie wind blow
good news and paper money into your hands.

When the carpet rises up
to meet your back,
may the dog welcome you with nips and kisses
to his good life on the floor.

Those days when the frost
lingers late on the greens
and your drives curve in unexpected ways,
may your putts glide like white fire
straight into every hole.

When your aching shoulders remind you
you've carried a long life's load,
may the power of your heart
sustain you like a twin-masted ketch
taking a long, smooth sail.

As old friends go away
without telling you when they will return,
may your children, grandchildren
and great-grandchildren
join to celebrate you and the never-failing love
you bestow on them all
like fresh rain on a sunny day.

Constant fiddling

"The self is the only history."
                               Ned O'Gorman

I am a place
in space.
I love myself
above all others
it seems
from the way I worry,
with my constant fiddling
with working out, with worrying
all the time about what to eat,
scheming about how to get
more money, planning
my heroically irresponsible
adventures when I
am finally free
to be —
to be the me
I know
I am
but can't get hold of it
and believe me
I try to reveal that me
in all its genius
of me-hood, me-be.
The me I see in the mirror
isn't all me, and
the one inside the body
I can't see or feel
all of either,
even in the mirror,
or a hundred mirrors
circling me, adoring

the ones who must be me
who, come to think of it,
is a you, too,
to you. I,
in that way,
am a you,
as you are a me,
essentially.

The cavern

Sound carries in places like this,
so, if you want everyone to hear,
speak in your normal voice.
But if you must say something private,
a personal confession, necessary gossip,
you're out of luck,
no matter how softly you whisper.
Secrets told here in the dark
ride the air currents up and out,
leaving behind the silence itself,
the ultimate secret no one can reveal.

The deal with the Angel of Cash goes bad

Look, pal. When you gave me the money
I didn't realize you'd get *all* my teeth
I know you're not in a big rush,
but will you wait till I'm through with them?
Who can make better use of them than me?
You plan to grind them into powder
to make a love potion for some little creep in Taipei?
She deserves it? And I don't?
Why does she deserve my teeth more than I do?
O, I get it. She's the bag lady who brings you her friends.
Why do you want her friends?
Just for someone to talk to?
You need an audience for your wisdom
or it wouldn't be wisdom, right?
If an angel speaks in an empty cathedral
does anyone hear? Not you.
You want someone to worship you
so you can laugh at them.
I don't need the money, not this kind of money.
No way I'm going to gum my chops for the next 30 years.
Stop by Friday, I'll have everything -
well almost everything -
all the money you gave me, in a box on my garage floor
I'll keep the souvenirs, the shells from St. Thomas
and the two goblets from the little shop in Paris -
she gave them to me, from her heart -
not like the business deal we made.
Yeah, I know it was your money that bought the tickets
but it didn't buy the love.
Come over after five on Friday,
I'll give it back and
from now on, I'll take my chances with your cousin
the Angel of Plastic.

Tender glances

in memoriam James Wright who wrote "Saint Judas."

A guttural
eye,
the one
wide open,
companion
of the other
tender eye,
half closed
in a wink of
teasing love.

Work long,
work hard
work free from
whatever it is
you doubt
could ever
hold you back,
hold you down,
hold you up
to the light

looking at you now,
old child,
my singer,
my song,
my other,
my me,
long gone.

The father's song
for Amy

"Oh, Dad, don't sing
that stupid song again."

She'd heard it at least
a thousand times
since she was born.

She hated the words about
how once you loved her
you could love nobody else.

She was afraid if
he kept singing that,
the only man who'd
ever love her
would be her father.

It wasn't true, of course.
But the truth is
no man ever sang
that song to her
with the lilt in his voice
the way her dad had.

Instantaneous evaporations

I was taking a shower and
watching a bird perched on the top branch
of the giant pepper tree.
I wondered if the bird
could see me through the window.
Soon, water splashed on the glass
and when I wiped it off,
the bird had flown.
This kind of thing happens to me
often. Like, when a bus stops
and I see through my greasy car window
a beautiful girl with black hair
wearing a green pompom skirt
or a noble old man with flowing white hair
and blue-lensed sunglasses
waiting on the street corner
and the light changes
and they disappear behind me
down the street. Or they cross
in front of the bus and I lose them.
I'm used to it now, what happens
when things change in an instant.
My dead friend called this
a world of mist and fog.
My living friend tells me
it's a world of streaky windows.

Small pleasure

I kissed her fingertip
goodnight.

Only her fingertip.

When the trees have fallen

When he was a young man
the old poet said
even when their trees
have fallen, birds can do nothing
but sing.

Is it song because we say it is?
Or is it more like
a simple sound made in hopes
some friendly creature
living nearby
might hear?

Weightless

for Ocean

When I carry
my infant grandson
and he's awake
looking around, fussing,
sometimes crying,
I say, "He's a chunk.
I won't need to
lift weights today."

When I carry
my infant grandson
and he's asleep
tucked into my chest,

I know how
a eucalyptus tree feels
the weightlessness
of a butterfly landed,
folding his wings,
clinging to a long leaf,
light as a breeze sighing
through the safe heart
of the winter grove.

Just before late September dusk

Margaret visiting from the Vineyard
She and Amy sit across from me
I face them from the bench in the bay window
They face me and the goldenrod-splendid
wildflower garden just outside the bay window
Margaret said, What's that?
I twist around to see her view
A small, maybe 200 pound black bear
probably a female,
strolling across the driveway beyond the garden
The bear stops and swings her head toward us
velvety fur darker than any starless night, shimmering
She can't see us, I said
But she knows we're here, Amy said
The little bear swiveled her head
back straight on shoulders
and padded off into the other wild meadow
where we used to stack the firewood
then she disappeared into the white pine grove
We sat still, wondering at her visitation
I said, They live down by the reservoir
My friend used to ride her horses there
They always shied,
spooked by bear scent
Our bear must be a female, Amy said,
She's only half the size of the big guy we saw
up above Deerfield when we were riding bikes
It was probably
using the driveway for a short cut, she said

Margaret said the bear frightened her
One of my friends, she said,
almost died when a polar bear
attacked him in his tent

They strung an electric fence around the campsite,
but the polar bear charged through and mauled my friend
That bear was crazy, I said
He must have been starving, smelled meat
Black bears are vegetarians, I said,
except for slugs and worms, mostly
This time of year
they won't bother you,
unless you bother them
or get between a mama and her cubs, Amy said

Later, Margaret had to bring in her pajamas
and toothbrush from the car
Can you turn on the porch lights, she asked.
I don't want to get eaten by a bear, she said, half laughing

Next afternoon, after Margaret left, we spotted
a golden-furred coyote on Grass Hill, east of the house,
less than half a mile from the Labradoodle kennel
our neighbors run, just up from the alpaca farm
down Adams Road

The coyote's mama must have been messing around
one night in the kennel, I said
Likely story, Amy said, grinning

The night we saw the golden coyote, the next night
at dinner without Margaret
Amy said, Last night at dinner?
It must have been heaven for you
You with two women you love,
when all of a sudden,
a bear saunters by, just after we said grace

Pride

Shirtless tonight at dusk
shooting hoops alone
in the shadows
on the desert asphalt court
below the sunset burnt
cliffs of backcountry Moab, Utah.
The keloid scar rippling
down the center of my chest,
a scarlet memento of
the night I ran and ran
as if I were a boy until
I collapsed on the high school court
far across the country. I came awake
to a helpless, breathing body,
the closest I've ever been to the spirit world.
When they masked my face
in the ambulance, pure oxygen
became my lover, my nurse. I watched the
digital numbers climb as my blood
sucked O2. At 100 the EMT smiled.
"Hundred percent. Can't get any better."
Eight years later, my breath coming fast
in the 90 degree heat,
the basketball slipped out of my sweating hands
and rolled away
into the hands of a ten year old girl.
She bounced it back, then turned
to her companion, a bulging blond,
saying, "Push me?"
She jumped squealing onto the swing
and the large girl pushed
the screaming little one almost as high as
the bar at the top of the swing set.

I turned from the children, dropped
a few more shots through the net,
and decided it was getting too dark
to shoot. I picked up my shirt
and phone and headed off,
leaving to the girls their private time
in the park. I doubt they cared
whether I was there or not,
a bald geezer with a red lighting
strike tattooed between his
nipples as ragged and smeared
as any other old tattoo
in this back country desert town.

I need my pills!

Pill bottles, empty pill bottles
littered the pharmacy floor.
Julianne stroked her kitten
while we all waited for the Roomba
to finish sucking at the tiles.

The pharmacy clerk said it happened all the time,
most often on Monday mornings
at the end of the month we're out of your pills.
When I asked if I could come back later
to pick up my prescription
she said, We'll give you a call,
tomorrow, maybe?

I need my pills
so, in a panic,
I called my doctor who said,
Don't worry. Go to CVS.
They have cases and cases of your pills.

I rushed over to the drive-thru
and called out my name and birthdate.
The clerk said, Credit card please.
I said I left it at home. Take cash?
Sorry, sir, we only take credit cards.
What will I do? I asked.
Come back tomorrow, she said.
But I'm gone tomorrow
and the rest of the week.

You could go home and get your card, she said.
We close at 9 p.m.
I looked at the dashboard clock. 8:46.
I lived 20 minutes away.
What time do you open in the morning?
8 sharp.
I'd be out of town by 8.

At home, Julianne said, Maybe you could
call a friend to bum a couple of pills.
That's how a lot of people do it these days.

I got on my phone, found a friend
with half a dozen pills – just enough.
I drive to my friend's house,
calmed down a bit, eager, hungry.

Paltry, the concerns of the self

The concerns of the self
feel paltry, like leftover grain
not even the chickens will eat
because it's gone moldy.
The paltry concerns are like
dust balls under the bed,
best to sweep them up &
throw them in the wood stove
& if you don't have
a woodstove, throw them into
the garbage bag where they'll
ride in the plastic to a landfill
somewhere not to rot
for decades, forgotten, never known
as more than a nuisance collection of fines
blown and tracked inside the house,
somehow bundling itself
into an object, a fragile
useless object, without a purpose,
a vague conglomeration
of puffed up micro-threads surrounding
nothing, & so an artistic
rendering, a sculpture based
on accidental adherence, a
synchronicity of dust, flowing air,
silence, darkness, all said
with respect for the delicacy
& bravery of dust kittens who
must be coaxed from their lairs
under couches and chairs
before they multiply & one day,
rise and roll
& somersault in the sun.

The money play

All this fury
about money.
I've never understood
money, or how
to get it,
never knew to keep it,
no matter how much
I wanted to.

That's capitalism
they say.
Keeping the dollars
on the move
is the only way
to make things happen.
Seems like cash
is an eternal immigrant,
a nomad,
a refugee from
my wallet.

I'm an actor
playing the role
of someone who could
make it.
It's not so hard.
I look around and see
everyone else
pretending
they can make it, too.

I pretend I know
what's up and what's
down and when
it will come around
in this keep-on-buying,
keep-on-selling
yourself, your-things,
your-time
world of ours.

I'm still acting
but the producers
have changed the script.
Now, they let me stroll
the boards and hit my spots
to my heart's content.
They tell me now
I'm in community theater
where the actors
do it for the love
of the applause
and to please the others in the cast.
It's called volunteer work.
The pay is in the good feelings
you get
from your hormones.

The light's so bright
on this stage
I can't see if
anyone's out there
watching in silence.

Is the silence
the silence of awe
or the silence
of absence?

I know for sure
at least one person
is watching.
Every morning he peers
out from the mirror.
He smiles
but I see through it.
I know acting.
The one in the mirror
can't convince me
he's real.
He's playing a role.
He's someone
who's barely awake.

Perfect

Perfect anything is like the steam rising off an autumn lake.

The swimmer, in up to her chin, her legs dangle free.
Floating at ease inside chilly water, watching the pines on
the shore hidden inside a gray cloud, the silence.

A minnow nibbles at her toe as she sweeps her legs back
and forth, then pumps her knees up and down to stay
afloat, without once marking the dull mirror of the water.

Time passes and the mist begins to thin and turn green
and gold in the sunlight rising over the land.

A few birds call as she climbs up onto the grassy bank.
A fish jumps, forming a bulls-eye of ripples
where she floated a moment ago.

Across the lake, the pines emerge from the fog.
Sun emerges through the leaves.
The grasses sparkle.

The drought, the city

In the year of the drought,
another drought, another year
when it rained on the next town over,
the city,
yes, the city took soft blows
of sweet steam on its chin,
unfurling its miles-long tongue
down to lap its own neck and chest.
The city never thirsted
in the year of the drought.
It knew steam would evaporate,
drips from ancient pipes
would never not flow.
With its tongue
like a child's twisty, curly
birthday party straw,
the city would never thirst,
unless the drought lingered
for years and years
and the sands move in to stay.

A dude didn't speak up

A dude didn't speak up when he had the chance
so the next best thing was to hightail it out of there,
find a safe perch
& watch the proceedings from above
then decide what moves he would make,
what help he could muster

until at last, he & his posse with their magical powers
rose up, fell back, rose, and fell, rose again
then swooped in
& took prisoner all his enemies,
locked them away for the rest of their lives.

Happy now, he sang a little song to himself
as he drifted off into his afternoon nap.

Polls

According to recent polls
around 1/3 of us say
we're happy.

The rest of us
would be,
if only....

Almost everyone's nervous

And it doesn't matter why,
says "I".

For each
& all
what matters
is

how well
"I" & we deal
with whatever
we agree
is the real.

Almost everyone wants

Almost everyone wants
more than they have
whether it's money
or a child
or a car
or a safe home
a mile from the hospital,
just in case.

Almost everyone knows

Almost everyone knows
less than they could,
even when they believe
it would help,
make life happier
if they knew more, like how to
fix the fan on the refrigerator
or how to bake the irresistible
gluten free chocolate cake
or tell a funny story
that makes people laugh
and keep laughing.

Almost everyone loves

Almost everyone loves someone
and then doubts her love
even when she hears
I love you
sometimes she doesn't feel
worthy of love herself,
because she needs
to be wrapped in her lover's arms
all night long
even when it's too hot to sleep.

i5 m1nuts b4 dawn

Sleepers wake, still adrift
across a bony river whose
clench in the storm shakes
vibrating ropes of muscle
and tender pillows of fat

and neither can
get enough of the other.

Illness or premonition?

The sudden lightheaded feeling
on waking
when you wobble down the hall
barely free of dreams
you already don't remember.

Leaving again

He's about to leave again.
Maybe this time he'll
stay away even longer.
She used to think of him
as always coming and going,
making trips down the highway
from country to city
and back and forth over and over.
He had a house he called a home,
a short-time home,
but it had all the furniture
and paintings hung and the light
he wanted in his home.
Until he left it.
Like he left the home before
and the others before that,
all of them falling
into memories like old print photos
piling up in a box.
He still carts the box around
from storage to storage
but doesn't open them these days.
So he's about to take off because
this latest home is finished with him.
In this life,
hundreds of millions of
nomads and refugees
shuttle across the planet
on our journeys and trips
without homes. Without homes,
it's the longing for homes we all have.

If we're lucky,
what we discover are places
to rest for a while
until the time comes
for us to leave
and search for home again.

It was getting late

It was getting late.
It was always getting late.
In fact, it was already late.
The shadows were denser
than they were earlier,
even those lengthening
on the lawn. It was late
but it had nothing to do with time.
People kept squinting at
their cell phones to see
how late is was getting.
When they saw what used to be
called The Time,
or What Time It Is,
they glanced up.
Always a glancing up,
some with disbelief
in their eyes, some with
smiles on their faces,
some with smirks
about the whole business.
It got later and later
until everyone sighed,
stood up, packed it in,
and went home to wait
before it got too late.

Saying something true
for Joebro

Usually, we let words
hint at
what we mean,
sometimes we say
directly
what we mean,
often nobody understands
the words anyway,
and maybe
that's the closest
we can come
to saying
anything true
at all.

Shattered

"Don't worry. I'll always love you to pieces," he said.

"There may be a problem," she said,
sweeping up shards of the shattered mirror.
"I'm running out of Superglue."

She's at large
for Honey

She's three years old.

It's the Long Beach Flea Market,
people everywhere.
People talking, people eating, people drinking.

She's three and
she's at large.
She looks around.
She sees legs, legs, legs,
moving slow or standing there.

Her brother and sister
haggle with a tsatske seller
over a necklace for her
and a knife for him.

She doesn't care about that stuff.
She saw it from up high,
when she rode her dad's shoulders,
but now,
she's on the ground.

She's three,
she's free,
she's on the loose.

She can't see her mom,
her dad's looking at his phone.
They'll find her if they try.
She knows they will.

Now, she's at large.
It's the Long Beach Flea Market,
people everywhere,
legs all around,
and she's on the loose.

She turns.
She runs.
She loves to run.
She's laughing.
She's three.
She's free.

Inishmore

He turned back signaling
with his crippled hand to come along,
join him in his morning stroll
through the ruins built of shining stone.
He knew the paths well
while you, in a lifetime of meandering,
have only just learned to see them
for the joy they brought people
instead of the griefs arising
from all the losses
you let sink out of sight
rather piling rocks and
raising bright stone walls
like the ancestors did,
not in defiance,
but from necessity
since rock and sky
were all they had to work with.

Mango, mango

Jamaican sunrise,
or was it Hawaiian?
dropped out of mango trees
as if to feed us on waves
and particles of the visible
but unknown
except what is formed
in the colored flesh of beings.
So we never knew
if the soul of things
was real
or something imagined.

To find out, we used science,
that is, theory,
that is, hypothesis
meaning a guess.
Then came the test.

We peeled the mangoes
and slipped our mouths
around the incarnate light.
Ah, the flesh dissolved
into sweet dripping juice
we sucked and swallowed.
Mama, we said. Mango, mango.

Sometimes
for Rick

Sometimes
when something common,
like water,
surrounds us
we feel surprised
at how calm
the day looks,
how smoothly
the waves flow
past our faces.

Sometimes,
when something
approaches us,
something amazing
we can recognize,
like love,
but we can't name
because we really know
only what we feel,

some gentle grace
lights up
with sun in the rain
a joyful hunger
everywhere in our bodies

and we surprise ourselves
with how we feel
at home.

Country songs

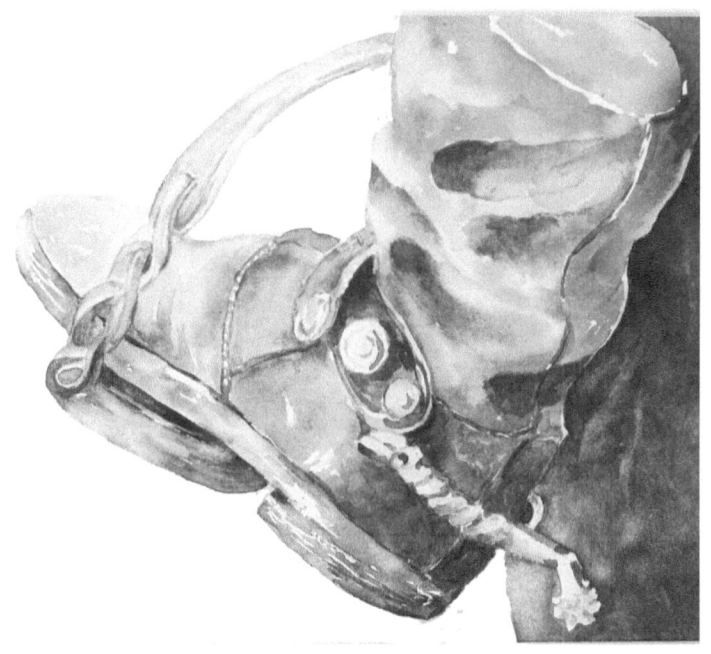

Ballad for Betty Ann

It wasn't the plan
it's ain't no joke
Betty Ann
had a stroke

path is crooked
path is steep
Betty looks
she's goin deep

woman's got brains
woman's got guts
rides the healin' train
no if, no buts

workin' hard
it can't be fun
out in the yard
here comes the sun

she gazes far, so damn deep
it's weird, it's strange
Betty takes the leap
time's gonna change

tough it is
new life's begun
humongous change
it ain't no fun

it's mighty hard
now it's spring
luck's in the cards
here comes the sun

Carousel magic spell
for Billie

Carousel
Tinker bell
Deep clear well
Magic spell

Truth to tell
Down I fell
Didn't land in gel
Magic spell

Dance pell mell
Wait to jell
Walnut shell
Magic spell

Nothin to sell
Magic spell
Never quell
Sing like Ariel

Fare thee well
Ride the El
Kokopell'
Magic spell

Maid in the dell
In love I fell
Tinker bell
Magic spell

Leaver

I've been the leaver,
I've been the left.
Ain't the one the easier,
Both some kinda theft.

I stole her heart and lost it
Way out on the road.
She ripped my heart to pieces,
I thought I had a home.

How could I be so selfish?
I knew just what I had.
Why could she never tell me,
What did she want so bad?

I've been the taker,
I've been the took.
We can't blame our Maker,
We ain't livin by the Book.

This time I know I'm smarter
Smarter than before.
Don't want just a good time,
Just a good time anymore.

I ain't in any hurry,
Only lonely now and then.
Still I wonder who
Might bring me love again?

Don't want to be the taker,
Don't want to be the took.
I don't blame the Maker,
I aint by the Book.

Don't want to be the leaver,
Don't want to be the left.
Either way I'm a griever,
Sure makes a lousy bet.

I've been the leaver,
I've been the left.
Ain't the one the easier,
Both some kinda theft.

I ain't packin' no gun

I ain't packin no gun.
Why should I?
You wanna carry a gun?
I wonder why?

My friend Wanda June
Lives in the hills up north a way,
She's a nurse, strong, smart, kind, too.
She came to see me the other day.

Wanda June, are you packin?
You bet, she said. I wondered why.
I don't carry no gun.
Why should I?

Don't tell nobody now,
She said, it ain't legal here.
Up where I live anyhow
Guns're everywhere, just like beer.

Wanda June, please tell me why
You're packin that heat.
You're safe around here, that's no lie.
No need to worry you'll get beat.

Wanda June said to me, You just don't know.
See that guy sittin right there?
See that bulge in his coat?
He's got a cold, cruel stare.

I ain't packin no gun.
Why should I?

Wanda June, I said, you don't gotta tote that gun.
Course I do, she said. I wondered why.
It's simple why I'm strappin.
I don't want you, me, nobody come to harm.
Don't you worry 'bout a thing,
She said, pattin' my arm.

I told you, my gun's my faithful one,
My pal, my secret beau.
I don't pack cuz he's warm or fun.
He's not for play, not for show.

Wanda June, it ain't love for you I'm lackin.
In the old days, I felt safe with you all the time.
Now, with you sittin next to me braggin about packin,
My life don't feel worth a dime.

She said, Take it easy, old friend,
I'll not be shootin you.
I'm loaded in case I need to fend
Off some creep, or save some kids, that's what's true.

You're all nervous, shiverin, you're afraid.
Heat's what you need, someone goes on a spree.
That's the whole story, she said.
Me and my 9 Milly, we're strong and free.

I still loved Wanda June.
Even when she came over hidin her gun.
But I said, Wanda, your packin here makes me blue.
Gotta go, pal, she said. Bein with you, it ain't no fun.

You wanna strap a rod?
Stash a pistol in your pack?
Nah, that ain't so odd.
It's kinda like bein' hooked on crack.

I don't carry no gun.
Why should I, what for?
You wanna pack a gun?
I don't wonder why no more.

I ain't packin no gun.
Why should I?
You gonna carry a gun?
Wanda June told me why.

A mattera

for Joey

It ain't a mattera
should or shouldn't
It's a mattera
do or don't

It ain't a mattera
would or wouldn't
It's a mattera
will or won't

It ain't a mattera
can or can't
It's a mattera
shall or shant

It ain't a mattera
up or down
It's a mattera
country or town

It ain't a mattera
what or why
It's a mattera
cake or pie

It ain't a mattera
below or above
It's a mattera
hate or love

It ain't a mattera
I or thee
It's a mattera
both you and me

Retirement nigh?

1.

Retirement nigh?
Easy as pie
That's a lie
You stop movin?
You stop movin

Love my bikin
Always hikin
Action's to my likin.
I stop movin?
I stop movin

In my brain, thoughts go throngin
My heart's filled with so much longin
And every day brings a new song in
You stop movin?
You stop movin

I like it high
I like it low
I like it on the go
You stop movin?
You stop movin

Bald is my pate
It's getting late
I know my fate
I stop movin?
I stop movin

Retirement nigh?
Easy as pie
That's a lie
You stop movin?
You stop movin

2.

I'd like to make a song
Not too short, not too long
Then give it to you, weak or strong
You stop lovin'?
You stop lovin'

I love my children
Grown women and men
I hug 'em any time i can
I stop lovin
I stop lovin

Who I want by me
We set each other free
Or climb up into a tree
We stop lovin?
we stop lovin

All I really want to do
Is be me with you
That's all I need, too
We stop lovin?
We can't stop lovin

I want you
You want me
A hug and a kiss and a tee hee hee
We stop lovin?
We don't stop lovin

The last thing I want
Before I say goodbye
Is see you, my star in the evening sky
We ever stop lovin?
No way we'll ever stop lovin

Suit you fine

Open your mind
plant a tree

Suit you fine
set you free

Right on time,
let us be

Going now
down the road

Ashes blow
heavy load

Didn't guess
I just knowed

Suit you fine
set you free

Open your mind
plant a tree

Right on time
let us be

Going now
down the road

Ashes blow
heavy load

Didn't guess
I just knowed

Home on the range redux

Oh, give me a home where the buffalo roam
Where the deer and the antelope play
Where seldom is heard a discouraging word
And the skies are not cloudy all day

O give me a home where happiness is grown
And children of us immigrants play
Where seldom we fear being sad and alone
And the clear skies are bright shining all day

The red man was pressed from this part of the west
It's not likely he'll ever return
To the banks of Red River where seldom if ever
His flickering campfires still burn

The red, brown, black, tan, white people are stressed
It's likely the west will continue to burn
With family and friends we all do our best
It's for peace and beauty we yearn

Home, home on the range
Where the deer and the antelope play
Where seldom is heard a discouraging word
And the skies are not cloudy all day

Home, home wherever we turn
And children of us immigrants play
Our hearts they will sing and freedom remain
And goodness is welcome to stay

How often at night when the heavens are bright
I see the light of those flickering stars
Have I laid there amazed and asked as I gazed
If their glory exceeds that of love

How often at night when the heavens shine bright
I cherish the light of those sparkling stars
I gazed there amazed and smiled as I praised
Their glory, the mirror of love

Home, home on the range
Where the deer and the antelope play
Where seldom is heard a discouraging word
And the skies are not cloudy all day

Home, home on the shore, the mountains, and plains
Where the children of us immigrants play
Our hearts they will sing and freedom remain
And goodness is welcome to stay

Look

Squirrel

Look: A squirrel untangles its tail
from a sapling's branches
then shakes the bird feeder
to rain his lunch onto the frozen grass.

Stone walls

Look: Down there, where the cars park,
weeds grow excited, ticks prowl the grass,
stone walls sag into the earth,
not caring they will never be skyscrapers.

Dreams remain

Look: Shelves bare, boxes stacked,
moving on, and still the dreams remain,
different than what today is,
and so what? Dreaming is for sleepers.

Enough

Look: Haven't you had enough
of this wishing, longing, praying,
or is that what sustains you,
your heart rhyming all day, all night?

Interracial

Look: Up and down the maples
a black squirrel chases a gray squirrel.
Today, an interracial couple
moved into the neighborhood.

Ladybug

Look: A ladybug, gauzy wings exposed
and trailing its round orange body
as it crawls across the window screen,
a slow comet against a blue sky.

Making something

Look: Her eyes downward,
not out of modesty or shyness,
no, she's making something with her fingers –
visions, feelings, truth-telling.

The night window

Look: in the night window,
a face, half-smiling.
Is it looking in
or looking out?

Not gonna do

Look: I'm not gonna do
what the old folks do —
scan the obits,
smile and say, whew.

Office stairs

Look: The stairs up to the office
rise like rungs on a ladder
propped against the wing
of a Piper Cub airplane, its motor revving.

Ridge

Look: A ridge of snow
rings the yard, piled
in merciless shadows
under sprawling pines.

The edge

Look: The edge of the winter pond
is free of ice. Clear water flows
through the culvert under the road
on the eve of my dead father's birthday.

Tufted titmouse

Look: A tufted titmouse perches
on the branch where the empty feeder
swings in the breeze. The bird lingers,
looks around, flashes off to the woods.

Voices

Listen: A voice says it's almost done.
Another voice says I want to sing.
Both voices sad, with longing,
sound like my friends, far away.

Little plant

Look: The little plant
casts its shadow on the wall
like a promise of soft seeing inside
where the winter sun reflects off a mirror.

No luck

Look: He knew he was finished
but he started again anyway,
aware there is no such thing
as luck, but, he thought, there is coincidence.

Family

Look: We're a family,
all families fight and abandon
each other. That's no joke.
But it can be funny in a childish way.

How else

Look: How else can we survive
if we don't romanticize
our failures and wear them
like shiny pelts on a sunny morning.

If they tell you

Look: If they tell you
what to do, especially
if they preach it or write it down,
ignore them – do what you want to.

Dark wingtip

Look: It's the dark
wingtip of winter,
rain pours down,
and we have no need to fly.

Work

Look: Somebody gave me work to do,
the Lord above or a little spirit or my mother
who said she'd speak to my father if I didn't do
what she said to do. So, I did and I do.

Quartz and granite

Look: You can't have the mystery
inside the translucent chunk of pink quartz
without the opaque history
of the mountain of granite.

Money

Look: You can get a job
and stick with it, if you need money,
or you can quit and go someplace else
if you don't.

Weather talk

Beside the beaver pond

Last week, it was
only last week,
wasn't it?
When corn shoots carpeted
the river bottom fields,
then we found ourselves
dreaming up at stars
as close as the ceiling
above the tunnel of towering stalks
we wandered through.
Now, corn stubble makes
a feast for crows and river gulls.
Where have the mystical flocks
of night swifts gone?
Where the herons?
Today it's raining.
The beaver family remains
in the river, hidden among their logs
upstream. Next week,
it will snow, and the week after,
if we're lucky, we'll be out
walking some night
when the beaver splashes
into the ice-scrimmed pond.
We'll stop and listen, then guess,
Is it he?
Is it she?
And weeks of walks after then,
when the corn shoots
arise all proud and chartreuse,

we, the walkers,
will walk and talk
quiet as the swifts' wings,
here now,
gone then,
back again.

Still playing basketball

At least I was
until one night
when my knee turned to cotton and my thighs
to Slinkys stretched flat.
I stopped running and shooting,
my animal forced
out of the pack,
the hardy young self I thought I was
grown older than I knew
or would admit.
So now, I walk.

Hey, Dad, my son said,
Are you limping?
A little, I said,
tho maybe it was a lot.
I walk on the edges of streets
where sand underfoot
cushions my steps.
The knee dislikes hard
and smooth paths, feels at home
trekking across roots or moss,
drawing strength from
wild earth or lumpy lawns
like in the times when play was all,
and the time after.

The night sips

The night sips at her bare heels
as she crosses the dewy yard.
When she reaches the front porch,
her feet pour up the steps,
her whole body a foamy rapids
washing across aged mahogany boards,
until it flows to the front door
where what's left of her
trickles into the house,
barely dampening the cool floor.

Two birds

Staying in the house of
my newly dead friend, his stone
sculpture paintings of
romping dogs and clowns
lit by track lights
over my bed,
I miss him,
our long talks
about the straw dogs named human beings,
our games of
pure five card stud –
no wild cards, no Chicago –
our long riverside walks.
So I pour his favorite scotch
he left in his cupboard
into a lonely glass,
& in his honor, I go outside,
splash some spirit
on his scraggly arbor vitae,
sit on his deck & sip
watching two robins in the yard.
One perches sentry
on a pile of pond rocks
my friend had heaped
for a someday sculpture,
while the other bird,
fat, deep orange on his belly,
picks at a wet black patch of soil.
Surreptitiously,
I scratch my ear.

The sentry robin notices and flees
into dark cedar boughs
& fat cock robin follows.
In an instant
I'm alone again
with the trees and my drink,
waiting for another friend
to come by
and sit with me
before we go somewhere else.

Clear pane of sky
for Noah

Beside a dawdling twilight river,
dusk floats in on
distant bird whistle,
fluid belling chirps and coos.

Rushing water tinkles,
gurgles.

High overhead
a clear blue pane of sky
surrounds haughty grey cumulus
thunderheads.

Miles south of the river bend
golden flickers
flash down a purple cloud rim.

Later, distant muffled rumblings echo
water's soft salutations to night.

Lanes

79th Street, New York, 6 lanes wide.
Adams Road, upstate, a bare two lanes.

You can walk them both.
The difference?

You cross 79th at the corner
avoiding careless drivers.

On Adams, you meander the whole pavement
avoiding careless drivers

and poison ivy on the roadside
under the trees.

Walking around
for Amy

She would still walk out across town,
a hilltown under dusty trees,
and out into an old forest
where novice hikers can discover
in dry silence a new kind of awe.

Still, she would walk
without thinking, noticing
she was on the move, only that,
because then her whole body
filled with longing for somebody

not to walk with her
but to be waiting for her
with food and a smile and
a question, not 'where have you
been?' or 'how do you feel? or

'want something to drink?'
none of those,
or all of those, and she would say
'it feels good to be here with you'
and he would say 'it's the way

I want to be me, with you.' Then
maybe they'd go back outside,
walk together, commenting on
cows or cliffs or trees or
how the river was muddier these days

so it must have rained up north.
Those were her lonely thoughts
those days, and nowadays, she walks
still, not as far, not every day,
and sometimes alone. She doesn't long
for who or what will be there
when she goes home,
She doesn't feel the longing
that used to pull her and drive her
every and each moment,
even as she drifted off to sleep
alone, not now, with him here.

How you become a bird
for Caraway

Beyond the dusty pane,
out the south window
in morning sun,
your eye lights on
a thin pine bough
fifty feet up
where you feel yourself
rock in the breeze,
until you shake and flit, drop scat,
and wing away
splitting the green air
in the invisible world
of branches and needles and shade.

The story of

The story of
the sore back
is the story of work

while the tale of
the sad heart
is the tale of weariness

and the fable of
the happy lover
is the fable of surprise

told over and again
in the saga
of the troubadours' songs,

the same saga beginning
when we're born into
this epic of survival,

beyond work, love, happiness
spoken as the plot
of faith rewarded

by the trust
we hold
in our belief

in the meanings of the tales
we tell ourselves
about our lives.

Snow

All the world outside the window
lies rimed and silent with new snow.

Now the wind rises a little,
the afternoon warms up,
and on the boughs and roofs,
the snow, giving up,
lets itself slide
down the branches and shingles
to the ground.

Plop.

Plop.

Christmas "Do"
by Jim

"Everybody sits around,
watches TV,
drinks beer,
eats.

Tries to burst."

Farmer's snow

"Might as well snow as rain,"
my farmer friend said one March,
"we can always use more white manure."

The sprouting of young narcissus
for Fiona

Late February.
Already the narcissus
shoot up in clusters
against the white wall.
Most of the town
called in sick this morning,
or stayed home to tend the ones
downed by flu or cabin fever.
Some of winter's exhausted snows
melt back from the house
revealing brown mud and
delicate little shoots
driving up into the icy air.

Listen to the narcissus speak.

Damn it. I don't care
if I'm early this year
or late. I'm back. I'm out
of hiding and don't you dig it?
I don't know how long I can
keep coming back
again and again like this – but
it's been years and
I'm still not tired.
Here I am,
sleet, snow, ice everywhere,
but so what?
You see me?

You should
learn from me.
Don't you just
love me for
how loyal I am?
How brave?
How green?

Shirley's brook

for Betty, Rick, Barb, and Joe

I named the brook after my mother.
The pond that feeds it
I named for my father.

The pond and the brook
carry on in the forest
at the bottom of Grass Hill

where my mother's brook flows to the west
before pouring into the swamp
below Nash Hill then gathers

with sister and brother brooks
slipping toward the river
running down the valley to the sea.

At the eastern base of Grass Hill,
the surface of the town reservoir
fell eight feet last summer,

so low the top of an ancient stone wall
emerged in the pond's center like the jagged back
of a mythical lake monster,

like a warning from the past
when the wall bordered a stream
before we built the dam

to capture and hold the water
for the townspeople's drinking,
washing, soaking, baptizing.

My neighbor's pond
down the road
dried up before the cow lilies could bloom –
the second time in 28 years, he said.

By October, my mother's brook didn't flow
from my father's pond, it trickled.
Then for a long month, it seeped.

Now, days after the first snow
just as winter begins,
my mother's brook flows again.

April, and now

And now the babies.

The yellow and purple crocuses long awaited.
The doves waking me in the morning.

Shovels in the garden waiting to work.

And the pear trees blooming in Brooklyn
raining fragrant petals on mothers and fathers.

A concrete bridge built for wagons
in a far gone day, now a path
through the woods to the garden.

Lacy carrot tips greening black soil
beside raspberries in Ashland.
And the afternoon light on the budding branches here.

Now you hear the babies' whispers
softer than northern light.

The owl calling in the dusk.

And now the bedtime stories.

Good Friday hike on Jesusita trail

Coming down the trail behind me
shrill college kids talking,
stop to ask me where they are.

I say you're on the other side
of the mountain from the Seven Sacred Falls.

Later, I follow them downhill,
through green brush where
spring mushrooms sprout
the size of forearms of three-year olds.

At a brook crossing near the trail head,
I crouch on a flat boulder
staring into the furry leaves
at the bottom of a tea-brown pool,
reading my fortune.
It says, "Love's on it's way."
I'm not surprised – that *is* the Jesus promise -
but there's more.
I hope there's something about money coming, too.
A cloud shadow ripples across the message,
darkening it. I squint to make out the meaning.
Then, the surface stills and the message is clear.
"Loves' coming. Forget everything else."
This bothers me. Am I losing my memory?
I turn to leave and,
making sure I'm heading in the right direction,
I hike downstream toward the car,
an oracle of peepers whistling up from the creek.

I stop, listen, sit down. It doesn't take long
before I start grinning,
remembering springs in eastern woods and wetlands
where I sat nights, letting the peepers
and tree frog symphonies-in-lust
jingle my eardrums,
their crazed songs chiming in the night temple
of the swampy woods.

Three and a half and mowing in the rain

for Ocean

Despite the rain washing down
from his yellow rain coat hood
onto his shoulders and hands,
intent on mowing the lawn
with the rusted green push mower
he found in the weeds,
the three and a half year old boy
tipped the mower back
on its roller and shoved it uphill
where he found a smooth
grassy patch so he
tipped the handle up and
the cutting blades down
and he pushed hard, spinning
the blades,
clickety, clickety, clickety,
clipped grass flying back
tickling his bare legs
while he laughed out loud.

Plants know

Now the horses have abandoned the land,
the boy who raised them grown up and old
and stricken with cancer, unable to mow
or care any more,

paddock and pasture gone wild
with Queen Anne's Lace, mock hemp,
pink clovers, while briars and brambles shove aside
alfalfa stalks the horses could count on all winter.

Bushwhacking, I follow fresh deer paths
to the top of the knoll, where slight breeze
cools my head. My eyes lift to the sky,
looking for a dancing partner among
plump cumuli lit gold at their edges.

As I head downhill, briar thorns stab
my bare legs, painting thin bloody trails
across my knees, reminding me once we stop
tending the earth with our human desires,

what was here before us comes back fast.
Plants know
the seasons of the earth belong to them.

May song
for Billie

Shy trillium
bow their lustrous heads
on a rainy
woodsy afternoon

offering walkers
who bend to peek
a sneak preview of earth's
blue eruptions

in violet petal

on indigo wing

in sapphire song.

Napping beside a summer pond

After dreaming of leading
the attack of swordsmen
and luring the enemy
into a screened gazebo
for truce talks
that ended in their bloody deaths,
I rose this morning at five,
never fully awake all day.
Already it's night again
and the crickets lull me down.

Before the storm
for Betty

Today, maple and oak
are stallions and mares
tossing their green heads,
their thick green manes,
high into the wind.
Tall grasses beside the road
discover that lawnmowers
fear them!
People ride bicycles home
from work smiling,
or cruise in big cars
munching the season's
sweetest strawberries.
And from the west,
from day's end,
wind speaks
to the wild herd of trees
in the distant,
insistent tongue of rain.

Another birthday

It's the birthday again,
another day on the calendar,
new brain and marrow cells abounding,
old cells sloughed off,
a selective memory ruling
a bright and sorrowful world
fading into nothingness,
rising again
through voices, rain, and longing,
hungers for joy and love,
all enduring
far beyond
the time anyone can imagine.

Fall

Around here nowadays
people talk about
sudden vivid changes
in the leaves overnight –

scarlet, gold, ivory, orange, chartreuse, maroon –

in the green forest,
down country roads and
along the streets in towns.

Milkweed

for Jasmin

In the fall meadow
where silence thrives
among grasses going dry
lie secret pods
whose love-seeds wait longing
for a fresh gust of wind
to shake and burst
and carry them away.

Autumn teases

Autumn teases
our senses,

pleases
our men's

and women's
souls, dense as

all that changes
and encompasses

you and me and us
and all of us.

October evening
for Barbara

Harvest moon grows round
above the cowbarn,
tenderly.

Cold air,
wet as matted straw,
hangs in shadows
laid against the shed.

Woodsmoke,
tangy,
drifts out thin
almost invisible
over the pasture.

Pushing back my cap,
I drink in the night

like milk.

Daylight saving

Frost clumps on the north side of
the pine needle piles in the side yard.
Chipmunks dash from under the stone wall
I lopped free of green vines and red sumac.
Now I've finished watching 3 years
of a TV series during October,
maybe I'll read novels again.
Or maybe I'll find another TV series to carry me
through night-blooming November.

Contentment

Fat little bobcat kit licking his chops,
rolling in the cool November grass,
fearless as only a young cat could be.

We watch him loll,
contentment incarnate
in fluffy gray fur,
his tall black- and white-striped ears
pointed straight up, on alert,
he turns and reveals
his white-ringed black-tipped tail
then stands and moves,
relaxed as a young lord,
or sleepy,
intrigued with some motion
under the deck where he disappears,

a rare visitor here in the woods
who can't be too far from home.

Surfing

for Danny

My son insisted he'd rather
surf the Rock
in the north Atlantic
in November
without a wet suit
than go to work at a job
he hated. "What about
hyperthermia?" I asked.
"What about asphyxiation?"
he replied. "What about
claustrophobia? Schizophrenia?"
I took out my handkerchief and,
always modeling good behavior for
my children, I sneezed into it. "Salud.
Gesundheit." My son continued
his litany of disease and I fell
into a pleasant trance like the one
you feel when listening to Gregorian
monks chant. "What about
carpal tunnel syndrome of the mind?
What about ischemia of
your loving heart? What about
deafness of the soul?
What about following orders
to the grave?"
I said, "Those are damn serious charges."
He sipped his Mexican beer and leaned close.
"What about dying in your
cubicle and nobody finds you
until they smell your body rotting?"

I stood up and dug
into my pocket. "Here," I said,
handing over my credit card,
"buy yourself a wet suit. Remember
to get a cap and booties, too."
He smiled and said, "Don't worry
about me, Pops.
Buy one for yourself.
When the water warms up,
you come on out with me
and give it a try."

Winter scene at a Pacific beach

The winter waves have scoured the beach of its deep
summer sand, raking it down and out and under the water,
leaving heaps of stones and shells, spreading
random smooth pebbles, sprawling kelp, and bleached
stumps and trunks in scatters across the dense winter sand.

Low tide reveals bleak, black bedrock tilted and tiered
in rows, like petrified waves, tarry ramparts protecting
the shore until spring currents shift the sand back inland
to buttress the crumbling bluffs in the dry season.

When I walk the winter beach barefoot, I'm an interloper
among the crowds of squatter stones. I move slow,
thoughtlessly timing my steps to the sounds
of the foam waves washing in and clear water rushing out.

My feet gliding across slimy, fly-mobbed kelp,
I pop amber kelp bubbles under my arches, releasing
the medicinal scent of kelp juice.
Last week, a sleek, ebony dolphin lay dead and glistening
on the beach like an abandoned angel fallen from blue
heaven. Groups of kibitzing humans gathered
and dogs sniffed at its inert majesty. In testament
to its celestial origins, the dolphin neither oozed nor stunk.

By yesterday, the gray and shredding body
lay on the upper edge of the beach, partially buried
under pale flotsam scruff. A lone seagull, so
single-minded it never glanced up when I came close,
hammered at dolphin meat with a stubborn golden beak.

I passed on by, heading up past where the dune
slid down in this winter's relentless rain.

Skiing the frozen lake

Skiing the frozen lake,
my mind wandering,
I remember the lively sailor girl
who took me out on the water here
one summer years ago,
wondering if she too
now has grandchildren
skiing and sailing
the waters
of our childhoods?

Buddhist Breathing in America

To the memory of Kurt Vonnegut
who hated guns

Ancestors' dreams

This place used to be called America
or what European humans –
the poor ones, a few brave ones,
desperate, hopeless, god-linked –
dreamed of, or so we're told they dreamed.

I suspect they had few choices
and strong imaginations
backed by guns,
backed by guns.

They lost everything
and their children roamed,
dirty, arrogant in their survival.
Some were grateful
as turkeys perched high up
in young pine

and these ancestors and their
not-so-precious children,
thinking they understood the maps
and playing the games they believed
they could win

wandered across what would be America,
confused in their ways and exhausted
and they slept,
waking this morning to what
used to be America

and still is,
backed by guns,
backed by guns.

Dirge for Afghanistan

The morning the crows landed in the yard
a fleet of black limousines passed the farm
following the patriot son back from Afghanistan.

The last day of September, the earth was hard
from no rain for months. Dry air felt warm
the morning the crows landed in the yard.

Dust rising all around, the limos inched toward
the hill, reluctant as soldiers to disarm
following the patriot son back from Afghanistan.

I leaned against the fence around the vineyard,
the tiny grapes drooping like a wizened charm
the morning the crows landed in the yard.

Twenty thousand bucks for school he'll never see,
a lousy reward. His mother wept with her head on her arm
following her patriot son back from Afghanistan.

Then the birds flocked up at noon, a midnight color guard,
lighting on the wire, perched in silent alarm
the morning the crows landed in the yard
following the patriot son back from Afghanistan.

Ode to Frank Stanford

I'm working to improve
my penmanship
so when you read
the words I write
they will enter your brain
as clear and clean
as three .22 caliber slugs
that entered Frank's heart
on the sunny day
that he laughed and called
"the last day of the rest of my life"
just before he wrote to his wife
"I'm glad you're not home.
I love you, baby,
but the goddam
pain's
all I feel anymore
and I don't want you
going down, too,
paying for the
morphine I
suck like a hog.
Besides, the dreams
burn my eyes.
I can barely see you now."
He sighed.
"So here goes, baby,
just like we agreed,
I'll stick around
in the ghost world
as long as you want me to.

Love forever ....."
and he drew the drapes
against a scorching afternoon.

Amerigun

O beautiful for spacious skies and amber waves of grain,
O terrible for specious lies and amber waves of shame,
For purple mountain majesties, above the fruited plain,
For purple mountain tragedies across the arid plain,
America, America, God shed His grace on thee,
Amerigun, Amerigun, God turned Her back on thee,
And crown thy good with brotherhood, from sea
                                                to shining sea!
And crown the hoods with brothers' blood
                                                from sea to warming sea!

O beautiful for Pilgrim feet, whose stern impassioned stress
O terrified the pilgrims' feet whose hopeful passions stress
A thoroughfare for freedom beat, across the wilderness.
The awful walls politicians beat and lost the wilderness.
America, America, God mend thine every flaw,
Amerigun, Amerigun, who could repair thy flaws
Confirm thy soul in self control, thy liberty in law.
Confirm thy soul in gun control when property
                                                is the law of laws?

O beautiful for patriot dream, that sees beyond the years
O sorrowful our immigrants' screams, their sadness,
                                                their tears
Thine alabaster cities gleam, undimmed by human tears
Thine addicts dream, our mother's flowing tears
America, America, God shed His grace on thee,
Amerigun, Amerigun, God turned her back on thee,
And crown thy good with brotherhood, from sea
                                                to shining sea!
And crown thy hoods with brothers' blood
                                                from sea to warming sea!

O beautiful for heroes proved, in liberating strife
O beautiful our heroes proved by losing precious life
Who more than self their country loved,
            and mercy more than life.
Who more than self their people loved
            but earned no mercy for their strife.
America, America, may God thy gold refine
Amerigun, Amerigun, please God your hate decline
Till all success be nobleness, and every gain divine!
Till everyone has open hearts
            and sees how every person shines!

Buddhist Breathing in America

I should have known better
but even if I had,
would I have stayed home that night?
How could I have stayed in,
the very day I learned
everybody
every day
breathes atoms
of the Buddha's eternally recycling body,
that same day I decided
to put on my good luck black pearl earrings
and take my breathing practice
into the suffering world,
the same day I heard the inspiring story
of the beautiful wife of the famous preacher
who loved him as much as a woman can
for more than thirty years,
giving him four children, four grandchildren,
stood behind his every preacherly and political move,
loving him while keeping her own identity as herself,

even when that beloved man
fell in love with a young widow
and made with her the baby
she and her now dead young husband
never got around to having,
and if that famous preacher
could make a baby with the young widow
when he helped her rebuild her life
because she was too young to grieve her youth away
and too lovely to avoid
the yearnings of men of all ages

and too weak to bear any love
but the preacher's
whose heart brimmed with compassion
until after hours of inhaling the pain of her sorrows
he came to know her as a woman of passion
whose fresh scent of longing intoxicated him
as if he were a teenage rector again
sneaking sips of the communion wine
after evening services,
and if he and that girl
could make that baby
and bring it home to his family and his wife
whose soul must have wings,
sharing it with his other four children
and their spouses and all the grandchildren

and if the beloved mother of all of them,
that pure, spiritual woman,
if she accepted that baby with open arms,
whom she had no blood tie with
so that new baby could
inhale her family's love
and then exhale its tingly baby breath over them
with purity and innocence that baptized them
with gratitude for life nobody could have predicted.

O yes, if that beautiful spiritual wife
and all her children could be so brave and accepting,
so inspiring, I could, I would, and I did
take my mindful breathing practice
out of my meditation room into our suffering world
by strolling down Beresford Street at eleven o'clock
one late August night
wearing my white flowered skirt
and my white cotton blouse from Guatemala

doing one after another after another
my breaths of compassion,
inhaling the unknown
and the spaciousness surrounding
the nothing from which everything arises,
exhaling the vapors of a star,
inhaling atoms so old
they were breathed by dinosaurs,
exhaling peace, light, and any relief I could offer,
ready for anything the void presented me,
prepared to know nothing about how to respond
to violence I might witness,
to drugs I might be offered,
to my own terror at being approached,
as I was, by three men who
demanded I come with them or
they would have to drag me
by my bitch hair.

O, I went with them
inhaling their desperation
and letting it mingle in my chest
with the roots of a raw scream.
I exhaled, unable to run because two of them
trapped me between them
and they pushed me into a garage
where I gave them my silver watch
and my crystal teardrop necklace
and they ripped my black pearl pendant earrings off,
slashing my earlobes open,

and I inhaled my own agony
like iron nails in my jaws
and exhaled musty relief when they cheered
the two hundred twenty seven dollars they found

in my purse before one of them shoved me
down onto the greasy, muddy floor
but not before he ripped off my shirt,
tearing it like paper in his grimy hands
while he slobbered on my neck with saliva
that smelled like cat shit,
and I didn't know what to do
so I exhaled the sweetness of light
onto his scabby head,
even when he pushed my skirt up
and yelping like a stepped-on dog
he yanked my panties down and dropped his pants
and lay on top of me and just lay there
waiting for something to happen,
I inhaled his decayed teeth breath
and I exhaled my wild heart pounding in my ears
and I gasped for air
and exhaled so shallow when

the other men laughed and said leave that bitch
we got what we want you
can't do it no way
so let's go
and they both spit on me
and the man laying on me grunting
and exhaling his excremental breath into my nose
slapped me and cursed me fuckin bitch shit cunt
and rolled off me
and staggered up pulling his pants on
kicking me many times
but I didn't feel anything
and he stumbled out of the garage

while I lay there
exhaling thank you thank you thank you

and inhaling the smell of greasy sour sickness
of heart and lung and clogged pores
and rotten food festering
in his tumorous gut
and exhaling peace and purity and light
and then I stood up wondering what to do
I pulled my long skirt up to my shoulders
so I was covered with a short dress,
and then nausea rose up into my head
and I bent and retched and retched
and I leaned against the wall
with my stomach clenching
until I pushed away and I dragged myself
back to Beresford Street shaking and shivering with
warm blood still oozing down my neck from
my shrieking earlobes

and I inhaled the garbagy scent of poverty
and the broken streetlight colors of shadows
and I exhaled the calm
of a damp, earthy garden
of tomatoes and corn
growing right there in a vacant lot
in the middle of the city
and I opened myself for the next thing
that would arise from the void
and still not knowing any better what to do
but feeling quite the blessed woman
inhaling and exhaling, inhaling,
exhaling,
inhaling,
exhaling,

I staggered home and climbed into the shower,
letting scalding water scrub his reeking touch

off my skin,
inhaling my coconut soap scent,
exhaling gushes of tears
until I fell soaking wet into bed
holding ice cubes against my earlobes
and sobbed and sobbed,
inhaling the sea scent of my tears
and exhaling my searing hate
for those creatures
who could have killed me
and I sobbed until I slept
and woke up and called Ronnie
and asked her to come over
and sit and breathe with me
 because my body wouldn't stop
shaking and shivering
until she came over and kissed me and
I inhaled her minty breath and
she inhaled my soggy ashen terror and
we breathed and cried together
and I hammered my fists into the bed and the wall
until I broke down laughing
and crying
and we rolled around on the bed
both of us giggling and sobbing

and then we got serious
and she bandaged my ears
her fingers tender and loving
and she held me for a long time and
first we breathed together until
we almost fell asleep in each other's arms and
we talked and talked
and I understood the world
in a new way and I decided

if I wanted
to give my breathing to the suffering world,
I'd better buy a gun and learn to shoot it
before I went out to Beresford Street again,
and I would,
I wanted to,
and I did learn,
thanks to those three rotting slabs of men
who tore tear tracks into my earlobes
I'll wear till I die,

I will be ever thankful because
I started shooting practice,
inhaling metal polish as I aimed and
exhaling fully before my finger
inhaled the trigger
so my hand stayed steady
as my pistol exhaled its deadly breath
and I ripped clean
heart shots again and again,
always inhaling the blue light of peace
and exhaling the dingy smoke of my own imperfections
of mind, body, and spirit
before I pulled the trigger,
calmly inhaling burnt sulfur fumes
and exhaling secret joy in my power,
concentrating on my aim,
hearing the crash of the shots pass
like galaxies being born,
watching the bullets eat a void
into the paper chests of my targets,

I became a Marksman
faster than any other man, woman,
or policeman ever did at the city range,

with a license to carry a Ruger P920
as naturally as I carry my phone.

When I told my teacher she said
The Buddha wouldn't kill.
I said I'm not the Buddha.
I'm good, I said, but the Buddha
is the deadest eye in the universe.
I can miss sometimes.
She smiled and squeezed my hand.
What about pepper spray? she said.
I understood but I was far beyond pepper spray.
I squeezed back and hugged her
and went home and searched the internet
until I found the best-selling Streetwise brand
Stun Gun on the market.
For fifty-nine dollars,
I bought the top-of-the-line model 10,000K Taser.
It looks like a cell phone but
one blast into the air at someone
and they fall to their knees
praying the lightning won't strike again.
And now I walk the city nights,
packing the Buddha's own sidearm,
one million volts of instant enlightenment
for the hungry ghosts and demons
who roam this city.

I walk endlessly, breathing in
any fumes the void presents,
exhaling my anger and fear,
inhaling all the stenchy and intoxicating scents
of this murky, sorry realm,
exhaling my loving breath into the eternal wind
that blows its perfume everywhere life is,

everywhere death is,
down on Beresford street
and every place else I may wander
in this rank and fragrant world.

Credits

Cover art by Deena O'Daniel
Photo of anonymous street art page 11 by Thomas Timmins
Watercolor "Cowboy Boots" page 81 by Maureen Moore
Photo "Owl" page 97 by Amy Timmins
Photo "Cyclone" page 123 by Danny Timmins
Photo "Beresford Street" page 163 by Thomas Timmiins

www.ingramcontent.com/pod-product-compliance
Lightning Source LLC
Chambersburg PA
CBHW030126260626
47156CB00008B/2813